The Firefighter's Obsession

EMMA BRAY

Chapter One

Zeke

MY HEART RACES as I stand on the street corner watching the smoke billow from the top window of the third-floor apartment of the towering building ahead. I can smell the fire and feel the heat radiating from the flames. I know that even from this safe distance, someone inside is in peril.

I'm technically not on the clock, but the way I consider it, I'm always on duty, so I run toward the building on instinct, hoping I can make it in time.

I'm a firefighter, trained in the art of rescuing people from burning buildings.

When I arrive, I'm met with the screams of a woman coming from the window of the third floor.

"Help! Help me!"

My heart pounds faster in my chest as I rush up the stairs. I have to be fast. Every second counts.

I run as fast as I can, taking two steps at a time, up the stairs and around the corners. I arrive at the third floor and see the room filled with smoke and flames. I can barely make out the figure at the window – a woman, standing there, petrified.

"I'm coming!" I yell.

I grab a blanket and wrap it around her, doing my best to protect her from the flames.

She's a tiny little thing, and she buries her face in my chest and clings to me trustingly.

"Don't worry," I try to soothe her. "I've got you."

I turn back to see that the way I came in is blocked. Out the window we go then.

Thank God the fire escape is still intact. I maneuver us through it and race us down to safety before something in the building explodes, as fires of this nature are known to do.

When we reach the bottom, I finally hear the sirens of my coworkers' truck sounding off in the distance.

I make a mental note to chew their asses out later.

Their response time was shit. If I hadn't been in the area and noticed the fire when I did, this woman probably wouldn't have made it.

I set the woman on her feet, noting that her head barely comes up to my chest. I keep my hands on her tiny shoulders to steady her.

Hair redder than the flames leaping from the building curls haphazardly around her face and falls down her back in long tresses.

I feel a strange tightening in my chest, and then she looks up at me with sky-blue eyes, and for the first time in my life, I have no words.

And I swear to God it's like the world falls out from underneath my feet.

Those eyes...

I've seen them before.

I've seen this exact same shade of light blue eyes staring at me from across a crowded room.

I've felt this same aura of familiarity, like I've walked this path before.

I've felt this before.

Maybe only in my dreams because I know this is crazy. I've never seen this woman before, yet I feel like I've just found something I've been looking for my entire life. Something clicks into place inside me, and my heart races in excitement.

I see people every day. I do my job, and I do it well.

I've never seen someone stand out as much as this woman does, though.

She makes my chest tighten, and it takes me a minute to realize why.

I've absolutely never felt anything like this. No one has made me feel so drawn to them before.

This must be what the old timers talk about when they say they found 'the one.'

"Are you okay?" I hear myself ask like the humongous dope I am.

She nods.

"I think so. Thanks to you," she says, those luminous eyes blinking up at me gratefully.

"Everything's fine now. You're safe," I tell her soothingly.

She looks up at me, and I see a spark of something flicker in her eyes.

"What's your name?" I ask her, needing to know it more than I need my next breath.

"Jaz..." she whispers, her voice soft and throaty.

But then she's ushered away from me by the medics, and as much as I hate to let her go, I know I need to let them do their job and check her out, and I have to lead my team in containing the fire and dealing with the aftermath of it.

With one more look over at Jaz, I head back into the burning building, firehose in hand this time.

I've got to put this fire out, and then I'll deal with the one that's suddenly taken blaze in the center of my chest.

Jaz...

My Jaz...

Chapter Two

Jaz

I CAN'T GET the firefighter's gray eyes out of my mind. They were smokier than the clouds created by the fire, yet I felt totally safe looking into them. Rather than suffocating in them, it was like I was able to breathe easier with them to ground me.

I'm sitting still while the medics look me over, mechanically answering the questions they ask me. They think I'm in shock, and maybe I am, but I'm more in shock of the handsome firefighter and his gray eyes than I am the fire itself.

I don't have a clue how the fire started. Someone in one of the other apartments must have started it, but I'm the only dumbass who took so long to awaken. I can't help it, though. I was exhausted after two back-to-back shifts.

It sucks trying to hold down two jobs just to make ends meet, but I'm barely scraping by even with both jobs. Sure, I could have kept staying with my stepdad, but it was becoming clear my room and board there would have come with a price now that I'm eighteen. My mom has been out of the picture ever since she died when I was fifteen. I was lucky he waited as long as he did before he started making his advances, I suppose.

But I'd rather take my chances scraping by on my own than deal with that.

I don't know where I'm supposed to go now. I have nowhere to turn but back to the stepfather I'm running from, so that's not an option.

I would rather be out on the street than back in that house with him.

"Hey."

That voice that soothed me just moments before suddenly caresses my ears, causing my heart to flutter faster.

I look up to see my firefighter towering over me. My heart skips a beat. He's got soot on his forehead.

He's covered in sweat, but his muscles bulge under the perfectly fitted tee he's wearing.

Those gray eyes are staring directly down at me, and I'm held captive by them.

"Hey," I answer back breathlessly.

He squats down before me so that we're eye level, and my breath hitches at the nearness of those smoky grays directly in front of me.

He lifts a hand and hovers it over my cheek like he's going to touch me before he curls his fingers in and pulls it back. "Are you okay?" his deep voice rumbles as his eyes rove over my face. "Did the medics check you out?"

I nod. "Yes. I'm fine."

He stares at me a beat longer, frowning as if he doesn't believe me.

I swallow, suddenly nervous, though I don't know why.

One of the medics who attended me comes up beside the firefighter and claps a familiar hand on the man's shoulder. "Hey, Zeke. Great job as usual."

Zeke. Mr. Smoking Hot Firefighter's name is Zeke.

Zeke never moves those gray eyes off me as he grunts a greeting to the medic, who then turns his attention back on me.

"I just need an address of where we can get in contact with you if we need anything further, ma'am."

I blink as that statement brings me back to the harsh reality of my situation. I look up at the charred apartment building I've been calling home for a few months now.

My stomach falls, and tears prick the backs of my eyes.

What am I going to do now? I worked hard to get that place. It wasn't much, but it was *mine*. A place of my own. Somewhere to lay my head at night.

My eyes drift away from the building to find Zeke's stormy eyes trained on me. He's staring at me with an intensity that makes my entire body break out in goosebumps.

Before I have a chance to answer, Zeke's deep voice rumbles, "She's staying with me."

Chapter Three

Zeke

JAZ LOOKS up at me with wide eyes, no doubt surprised by the forcefulness of my statement.

But I meant it. This girl is staying with me. No if's, and's, or but's about it. There's no way I'm letting her walk away from here with no place to go. Not when I'm more than willing to protect her.

"Are you sure?" she asks me in that pretty little voice of hers, her blue eyes looking so innocent it hurts to look at her.

I'm a filthy fucking bastard for the images that run through my head when she looks up at me like that. Her on her knees in front of me, my cock between those puffy pink lips, her eyes looking up at me just like that...

Fuuuck...

I push the thoughts aside and focus on the task at hand. "Yeah, I'm sure," I tell her with a quick nod, hoping she doesn't see the lie in my eyes. I'm not sure about shit. Well, I'm sure about one thing, but I'm fucking unsure about the rest. It's been a long time since I had anything good in my life. Any happiness.

And I can't help but feel like this girl is going to be the one to change everything.

"Well, I'm sure you'll have no issue handling her relocation," the medic says with a smirk.

I glare at him until his smirk fades into a look of uncertainty. Never mind the fact that he's right, I won't stand for anyone making insinuations about my girl.

I'm sure I will have no problem taking Jaz to my place, fucking her brains out...

Just the thought makes my cock twitch in my pants and my hands clench at my sides.

With a growl, I turn back to Jaz.

I grab her hand again and pull her toward me, my hand wrapping around her small wrist. I can feel her pulse drumming at an erratic pace beneath my thumb, and I watch as goosebumps break out along her delicate skin. I'm sure it's from the cold, but it could just as easily be from the way I'm looking down at her, my eyes devouring every inch of her body.

"Jaz," I whisper, the sound of her name leaving my lips making her tremble beneath my touch. Her eyes slide closed, and I lean in closer to her, my lips brushing against her ear when I say her name again.

"Jaz," I say with a little more force this time, and her eyes flutter open, locking onto mine as a shiver runs through her.

"Let's go," I say, my voice so low it's a whisper.

I don't wait for her to answer.

I pull her to a waiting cab. I hold the door open. Jaz slides in, and I follow closely behind her, crowding her so that her little body is slammed into my side.

The scent of her shampoo fills the cab, mixing with the leather and the familiar smell of the smoke staining my skin.

I bark our direction to the cab driver before I turn back to face Jaz, my eyes locking on hers as she looks up at me, her cheeks flushed and her lips parted.

She's fucking beautiful.

"Are you sure?" she asks again, her voice still breathy.

"Positive," I assure her once again, my hand coming up to cup her cheek. Her eyes widen, and I'm not sure exactly what she's thinking, but I don't let her answer. I lean in, burying my nose in her neck and breathing her in. Fuck, she smells like heaven.

It's too fast, but I'm not in control of my actions. Everything in her is calling to me.

I kiss her neck, my lips brushing against her soft skin, my fingers tangling in her hair and pulling her toward me.

She gasps when I pull her so that she's straddling me and grind my hips against hers, humping my erection against her.

And that's when I know that she's *mine*.

I don't care what she says.

I don't care if it's been a while.

I don't care if we've only known each other for a couple of days.

I've never felt like this about anyone.

I'm not going to let her go.

Jaz

I should be worried.

I should be freaking the fuck out.

I mean, let's face it. I'm in a cab with a firefighter who's a veritable stranger to me.

I don't know him.

But something about him...

No, something about us...

Us?

I'm not fucking thinking about that now.

Something about him makes me feel like I can trust him.

I *want* to trust him.

And that's all that matters.

I should be worried.

Hell, I *am* worried.

But I'll worry about everything later.

I'm very aware of the way he wraps his arm around my waist and the way he pulls me to him when he kisses my neck.

The way his cock hardens when he grinds his hips against mine.

His breath on my neck.

Inhaling my scent.

Tangling his fingers in my hair.

Claiming me.

My lips part. I've never been kissed before, but my lips are tingling in anticipation of this man's kiss now.

I've completely forgotten where we are. It doesn't matter that we're in the backseat of a cab. The cab driver is nonexistent.

All that exists in this moment is Zeke and me.

But then the cab comes to a stop.

Zeke pulls back from me with a groan, but the clouds in his gray eyes are rolling harder than ever. The intensity I see there takes my breath away.

They're full of promise of what's going to happen between us if I just let it.

If I just let *him*.

I *want* to let him.

"Jaz," he croaks out my name, his voice full of lust.

I blush and scramble off him. He hands the cabbie a hundred-dollar bill and tells him to keep the change.

Zeke ignores him. His attention is already back on me. He grabs my hand and helps me out of the cab.

He keeps my hand in his as he leads me to his apartment.

I feel like I'm being pulled toward him by a force stronger than gravity. My body gravitates toward his, magnetized.

I'm going to follow him wherever he leads me.

"Are you okay?" he asks as he pulls me into his apartment and kicks the door shut behind us.

"I'm fine," I lie. I'm not fine. I have nowhere to live

now, and the feelings this firefighter are stirring in me have me confused as hell.

Zeke lifts my chin to look me in the eyes and traces his thumb over my jawline.

"I've never met anyone like you."

I can't speak. All I can do is stare up into his mesmerizing gray eyes.

"Jaz," he croaks out my name again, and I swear to God the sound is like coming home.

And then he kisses me softly, gently.

He kisses me like a man in control. He kisses me like he knows what he's doing.

He kisses me like he knows what I need.

He kisses me with a forcefulness that takes my breath away.

His lips are firm on mine, but they're so soft. He kisses me over and over again and I whimper, wishing I could get closer to him. Wishing I could get all of him.

I move my lips against his as he gives me what I need.

I've never felt anything like this.

I've never felt anything so nice before.

My body breaks into goosebumps as he claims my mouth with his.

I want to be taken by him. I want him to give me

everything he has.

I want him to take me to another world. I want him to take me to a place I've never been before.

I want him to take me to his bed.

I want to be with him.

Zeke groans as his hands move to my hips.

He pulls me against him, and I gasp at the hardness I feel there.

He wants me. He wants me just as badly as I want him.

"Fuck Jaz. What is it about you, sweet girl? You've got me all fucked up."

My heart skips a beat at his words.

"I have to have you," he growls before he claims my mouth again.

"Yes," I moan into his kiss, not caring that I just met him. All I care about is how his lips feel so right against mine, how safe I feel in his arms. It doesn't make sense, but it doesn't have to. I want this. I want *him*. "Yes."

I reach up and grip the back of his neck, pulling him even closer to me.

He steps forward, pushing me backward until I'm up against the wall.

He kisses me fiercely, his tongue forcing its way

into my mouth. He swipes his tongue against mine and I taste him, tasting a man for the first time.

His hands move to my breasts, and he slides a hand under the edge of my shirt, brushing his fingertips against my bare skin.

The little sparks of pleasure he creates are enough to drive me insane.

"You taste so fucking good, sweet girl. I can't believe how good you taste," he growls into my ear.

I follow my instincts and reach down and squeeze his cock, my eyes widening at the size of it. It feels massive in my hand, and it's a wonder I'm not scared.

But I'm not scared. I want him.

I want him so badly.

He groans and thrusts his hips into my hand before he pulls my shirt off over my head and moves his lips down my throat, kissing and sucking. Each touch of his lips on my skin sends a shiver down my spine, making my need for him that much more intense.

When his lips reach the swells of my breasts, my heart rate spikes.

He sucks my nipple into his mouth and nips at it lightly with his teeth. I gasp as he takes my nipple between his teeth and tugs.

"Oh my god," I moan as I lean my head back.

"Sweet girl, you should see the way you look. Pure fucking perfection," he groans as he moves to my other breast and sucks the nipple between his teeth.

My body breaks out into goosebumps again at his words. It's not often that I feel beautiful, but when he looks at me, I feel exactly that.

He moves his mouth down my stomach again. He moves lower until his lips are at my belly button. He kisses around the belly button before he dips his tongue inside.

And then I feel his tongue on my clit.

I moan his name again as I grip his hair. He sucks my clit into his mouth, and I feel his tongue flicking against it.

I grind my pussy against his mouth, wanting more. His tongue is magical, sending me closer and closer to my orgasm.

"God, your taste is amazing, sweet girl. I can't wait to taste every inch of your body," he growls into my pussy.

He dips his tongue back inside my pussy and flicks it against my clit, sending fresh bursts of pleasure through my body. I'm already so close, and his tongue is just driving me higher and higher toward the brink of my orgasm.

I feel my legs shaking uncontrollably as I get closer

and closer to my climax. I feel like I'm about to burst.

I place my hand on his shoulder, steadying myself against it. I find it hard to breathe as I lean my head back and groan his name.

"Zeke, please!" I beg him.

He moans into my pussy as he licks me faster and dips his tongue inside me. The sensations are too much, and I explode. My whole body shakes as I come against his mouth, moaning his name. My orgasm goes on and on, and when I come down from it, he's standing up in front of me again.

He kisses me wildly, his tongue fighting its way into my mouth. I can taste my own juices on his lips.

He kisses down my throat to my breasts and pinches my nipples between his teeth again. The sensation of pain mixed with pleasure has my pussy throbbing again. I can feel myself getting wet again, and I know that I won't be able to take much more of Zeke before I'm a puddle at his feet.

"Zeke, please," I beg him.

A rough growl escapes his lips as he moves to stand in front of me again. I feel his fingers slip inside me, and then he's moving them out. I watch as he brings his fingers to his mouth and sucks them clean.

I bury my face in his shoulder, embarrassed. I've never done any of this before. I've never had anyone taste themselves off my body. It's sexy, and I feel so many emotions at once. I feel embarrassed, turned on, and aroused.

The truth is, I want him just as badly as he wants me. I want to feel him inside me, driving me wild with pleasure. I want him to make me feel good and to make me his, and that realization gives me courage.

"Fuck me, Zeke," I whisper into his ear.

He makes a strangled sound at my words and looks down at me.

"Please," I beg him. "I want you so bad."

He grabs my face between his big hands and speaks directly against my lips. "You don't know how much I want you right now. I want to bury my cock in your sweet cunt so bad, Jaz," he groans.

I run my fingers down his chest and lower them until my hand is on his cock again. Holy fuck. My eyes go wide as I feel just how big he is. Somehow, he's gotten even bigger than he was before. I can't imagine that he'll fit inside me, but I want to try.

"I'll be gentle, sweet girl," he promises me.

"I know," I whisper back.

He guides my body down to the bed and pulls my hips up to his. I can feel the head of his cock nudge my entrance and then he's pushing into me. I can feel the rawness of his movements as he tries to restrain himself, moving slowly but forcefully, burying his cock in me.

I feel a pinch of pain, but he keeps going until he's all the way in me, and it's more than I can handle. It feels so good, and I feel like this is what I was meant to be doing.

I whimper at the sudden fullness inside me.

He starts to pull back, his cock nearly coming out of my body, but I want more. I want him to fill me up, to fuck me hard and rough. I wrap my legs around his waist and hold him there.

"More, Zeke. I want all of it," I beg him.

I hear him growl in approval, and he pulls back, slamming into me again. I cry out as pleasure beams through my entire body. I can feel his cock pulsing in my pussy, and I know that he's going to come soon.

I don't know if he can feel it or not, but I'm about to fall apart. I wrap my arms around his neck and hold on as he pummels into me. He's hitting me at just the right angle, hitting me in all the right places, and when I come I'm screaming his name.

He keeps pounding into me, until he groans and buries himself as deep in me as he can go, his hips jerking against mine. I can feel his cock spasming against my walls, and everything becomes a blur.

"Oh, fuck, Jaz. I can't get enough of you," he

groans as we both come down from our highs. He strokes my hair as we catch our breath.

I don't know where we go from here. I don't know how I'm going to be able to face him tomorrow, or the day after that, but for now, I just want to bask in the glow of pleasure that I feel.

Chapter Four

Zeke

I'M DOING IT AGAIN. I let her sleep for about an hour before my body demanded I claim her again.

I'm holding her in my arms, telling her how much I want her and how good she feels, and I'm going to fuck her all over again.

I lay her on her stomach, her long red hair flowing out around her. I watch her body shift and move as she tries to get comfortable. I don't think I'll ever get tired of looking at her or holding her in my arms.

"Do you have any idea how beautiful you are?" I ask her as I run my fingers down her back.

I flip her so that she's laying on her back and run

my hand down her body, from her neck over her breasts, down her stomach and over her hips.

"I want to make you feel good, Jaz. More than you can imagine," I whisper against her skin.

God, she's so fucking soft. She's perfect. In every way.

I take my hand away from her, and she lets out a whimper of protest. I run my finger down the side of her face, then lean in and kiss her under her ear. I nip at her earlobe.

Her breathing picks up, and I can tell she's ready for me again.

And I'm always ready for her. My cock is leaking a steady stream of precum. I didn't know my body was capable of making all the cum it has since the moment I set eyes on Jaz. My chest swells as I look down at her, and then words come tumbling out of me. I can't stop them.

"I love your body, Jaz. I love how you feel against me. I love the way you sound when you come. I love the way you feel when you cum on my cock. I love your smell, your taste, your soft skin and your gentle curves."

She's looking up at me, her mouth slightly parted as I confess my insane truths to her.

My heart is beating a mile a minute. I sound like an obsessed psycho, but she's not running.

I lean down and kiss her deeply. She's getting even wetter. Fuck, she *likes* what I'm saying to her, and something about that drives me even wilder.

"I want you, Jaz. All of you," I whisper, then take her completely with my kiss. I lay myself over her, my body pressing into hers. She arches her back, and I feel her breasts brush against my chest.

I run my hands over her body, lingering on her breasts, her hips, and her ass. I grab her ass cheeks in my hands and squeeze them, pulling her harder against me. At the same time, she's grinding her pussy against me.

I'm so hard I can barely feel my own body. I look down at her again and almost come from the sight of her. She's so fucking beautiful with her lips swollen from my kisses.

I roll off her and settle myself beside her.

"Come here, Jaz. I want to touch you. Let me feel your body against mine."

She moves toward me, and I pull her tightly against me. I run my hand over her back, her shoulders, her breasts, and her stomach. I pull her leg up so that it's over my thigh, then I run my hand over her hip and down her leg.

I can feel her wetness again. She's ready for me.

I don't know what I'd do if she said no right now. I have no control over my body. I have no control over my actions. I have no control over my words.

She nuzzles my neck and runs her fingers through my hair.

"I want you inside me, Zeke. Fuck me. Please," she moans.

I want to scream in triumph, but I just start kissing her. There is no triumph, no victory, only her.

She raises her hips, and I slide inside her. I groan. It feels so fucking good.

"You're so tight, Jaz. I love being inside you," I tell her.

"This feels so good," she murmurs, then runs her tongue over her lips.

I'm in heaven. I can't believe this pretty little thing wants me as much as I do her.

I lift her hips again and start moving in and out of her. I want to make love to her until neither of us can move.

"Oh, Jaz. Fuck, you're so sweet. I love being inside you. I love touching you," I breathe as I kiss her lips and her chin and her neck.

She moves faster against me, and I feel myself

coming closer and closer to the edge, but I don't want to come yet.

I make a strangled sound. Too good! She feels too fucking good, and I'm about to lose it.

"Jaz, baby," I growl. "You've got to slow down, honey. I'm so close, but I don't want to come yet," I beg, then pull her tightly against me and kiss her tenderly.

She opens her eyes and looks at me with a question in her gaze.

"I want to make this last as long as possible. I want to make love to you all night," I tell her.

She runs her hand down my side and squeezes my ass.

"Fuck me, Zeke. Make me come. Please..."

How could I ever tell her no, especially when she begs me so prettily?

"I could never say no to you," I confess before I bury myself deep inside her and start a slow rhythm, moving in and out of her.

Each stroke pushes us closer to the edge. I want her to come with me.

"Zeke!" she begs. "Don't stop!"

"I'll never stop, Jaz. I'm going to make love to you all night. I'm not going to stop until you come. And I won't even stop then. I'm going to keep you coming on Daddy's cock all night long."

Jaz's eyes snap open in surprise, but I feel her pussy clench around me at my words.

I don't know where the fuck that came from, but I'm not taking it back now.

"That's right," I growl against her, suddenly even more turned on at the thought of being this girl's daddy, the one she comes to with all her problems, her protector, the one who's going to take care of her. "I'm your daddy now. You know it too, don't you, sweet baby?"

I move faster and faster, my cock swelling bigger and bigger.

"Oh fuck, Jaz, baby, baby, baby." I'm chanting her name and spewing nonsense. I can't stop now. I couldn't stop now if my life depended on it.

I feel her getting closer and closer. "Come with me, baby," I encourage her. "That's it. Give it all to Daddy."

"Zeke!" Jaz screams as her pussy clenches down on me hard and tight.

"Fuck!" I roar out my own climax as her cunt muscles milk me for all I'm worth. There's no way in hell I can hold back with her pussy falling apart on me like this.

I turn my face into her neck and breathe in the scent of her skin as I spill my seed deep inside her. We collapse on the couch, panting and moaning as we slowly come down from our orgasms.

I kiss her, and she kisses me back, our tongues tangling lazily together. I tighten my arms around her, my chest flooding with possession.

Mine. She's mine.

I want her with me, at my side. Always. I want to take care of her, protect her, and take the pain away from her.

Neither of us speaks. Neither of us wants to talk about what's going to happen or where we're going to go from here. I literally just met her tonight, but I feel like I've known her a lifetime.

And that's all I need to know.

As far as I'm concerned, Jaz is going to stay here with me forever.

I'll worry about making her see that in the morning.

For now, I pull her tight against me and stroke her hair until she falls soundly asleep against me.

Mine.

Chapter Five

Jaz

I AWAKEN SLOWLY, and it takes me a few seconds to realize where I am.

"What the--?" I mumble as I blink my eyes open. I glance at the clock. It's eight o'clock in the morning, and I'm already late for work.

I'm going to be in so much trouble. I quickly sit up and look around, but Zeke is nowhere to be seen.

"Zeke!" I call out, suddenly panicked at the thought of being alone without him.

"Up here!" I hear Zeke's voice from upstairs—the part of his apartment I didn't get to see last night since we never made it beyond the bedroom. "Come on up!"

"I don't know if I should!" I call out as I climb out of the bed. "I'm already late for work."

"It's alright," he calls back to me. "I just have to show you something."

"What?" My curiosity is instantly piqued.

"You'll understand when you get up here." I frown at his evasive answer before I start to climb the stairs toward his voice.

"Good girl," he whispers.

We're the only two people here, so I don't know why he's whispering, but the sound sends a shiver of desire down my spine. God, what the man's voice does to me when it's all husky like that.

"Turn left," he instructs me. "Don't come in the room. Just peek in."

I do as I'm told, but I can't see anything.

"Zeke?" I ask.

"It's a surprise," Zeke laughs. "Come on in."

I move tentatively into the room. Still, though, I'm a little confused when all I see is an empty room. "Why do you want to show me this room?"

"Because it's yours."

I stop dead in my tracks.

"What?" I try to comprehend his words.

Zeke crosses the room and takes my hands in his, his gray eyes boring into mine with so much intensity it takes my breath away.

He gently squeezes my hands. "I want you to stay with me. You don't have to worry about anything anymore, baby. I'm going to take care of you. And I want you sleeping with me in my bed, but I also don't want you to think that's all this is, so I want you to have a space all your own. I know how important that is to you."

Tears well up in my eyes. How is it this man gets me better than anyone I've ever known and I've scarcely known him a day?

"Zeke, I..." My throat tightens, and words fail me. I don't know what to say.

"This is where I want you to live...with me." His eyes are probing me with that stormy intensity that takes my breath away.

"Zeke..." I shake my head, overwhelmed. What should I do? Part of me wants to accept his offer, but that other, independent part of me tells me that I have to make my own way.

"I have to go to work," I finally croak out. "I'm late."

Zeke cups my face in his big hands. He shakes his head. "You don't have to work anymore if you don't want to, baby. Don't you get what I'm telling you? I'll take care of everything if you just let me."

I lick my lips nervously as I stare up at him, unsure.

"What do you say, Jaz?"

Zeke's eyes are pleading with me to accept, but still, I hesitate. I'm not even sure why I do. Maybe it's because everything is happening so fast, and it all seems too perfect and I'm not used to anything in my life being so perfect or effortless.

It almost makes me afraid that this is all too good to be true.

Before I get a chance to answer him, his phone rings.

Zeke frowns as he pulls it from his pocket and answers it. His face changes in an instant as I see him go into firefighter mode.

I already know that he's going to have to respond to an emergency before he hangs up the phone.

"I'm sorry, Jaz," his eyes are apologetic but determined, "but I have to go. I'm on call."

I shake my head. "No, it's okay," I assure him. "I get it."

He presses a swift kiss to my forehead before he heads for the door.

"Please be here when I get back," he calls out over his shoulder.

I don't answer him. Instead, I just wrap my arms around myself and watch him disappear, wondering why I suddenly feel so empty—as if he's taken a piece of me with him.

My first job is waiting tables at a local diner, and I have to endure the glare of the manager when I come running in the door nearly an hour late. I ply him with the story about how the apartment I lived in burned down, but he has no sympathy for me. He just barks at me to get to work and not let it happen again.

Yes, sir.

I'm just grateful he didn't fire me on the spot because I cannot afford to lose this job. Never mind that I have another job cleaning the hospital after this one. I need both to make ends meet.

That thought causes me to pause. Well, technically, I guess I don't need both jobs anymore—if what Zeke said is true. If he really wants to take care of me. If he really means it when he says he'll handle everything and I don't even have to work.

Of course, I'm not the type of girl to take handouts, and it goes against everything in me to imagine myself not working and letting someone else do everything. I want to pull my own weight.

Still, it takes a load off knowing that there's someone else there to share the burden now. I don't feel as stressed as I normally do.

But I'm not going to take advantage of Zeke's charity. I'm going to keep both of these jobs and pay my own way. Even if I do take him up on his offer to stay with him, I want to contribute something.

"Jaz," a voice that causes my blood to run cold stops me in my tracks.

I turn around to see my stepdad frowning and leering down at me all at once.

"Jeff," I squeak. What is he doing here? How did he find me?

I haven't seen him since I fled his house in the middle of the night and never looked back.

He's been the bane of my existence ever since my mom brought him into our lives, but at least I haven't had to deal with him since I left.

I'm hoping that I can keep it that way.

He's tall and lanky with a face that's starting to sag with age. He's got thinning black hair, and he's dressed in a suit that's much too nice for the diner. I guess he's not working today—just trying to find me, probably.

"Where have you been, Jazzy?" he asks, his voice almost singsong-y as he calls me the nickname that makes me grit my teeth. I always hated it when he called me that. "I've been looking all over for you."

I clench my jaw and refuse to look him in the eye.

"I'm at work, Jeff," I tell him, biting my tongue to keep myself from calling him the bastard he is.

He's the reason I ran away from my home and the reason I'm working two jobs to support myself.

"You can't just run away from all your responsibilities, Jazzy," he snarls at me. "I need you home."

I back away from him, feeling my heart beating faster in my chest. I don't want to be near him, but he steps closer to me, invading my personal space.

"You're not taking care of your stepdad like you should be," he continues, his breath hot on my face. "You're neglecting your duties as a daughter."

I shake my head, trying to push him away from me. "I'm not going back with you, Jeff. You can't make me."

He grabs my arm, his fingers digging into my skin painfully. "You don't have a choice, Jazzy. You're coming with me."

I try to fight him off, but he's stronger than me. He

drags me toward his car, and I know that I'm in trouble.

As he shoves me into the passenger seat, I catch a glimpse of Maria, my coworker, through the window of the diner. She looks concerned, and I know that she's seen what's going on, even though I know she's helpless to help me.

Jeff gets into the driver's seat and starts the car. I'm trapped, and I don't know how to get out of this situation.

But I know that I can't let him win. I can't let him control my life again.

I take a deep breath and steel myself. I'm going to fight him every step of the way, and I'm going to come out on top.

I lunge for the door, but he locks it before my hand ever reaches the handle.

I raise my fist, ready to smash it through the glass to get out, but Jeff's next words stop me.

"I wouldn't do that if I were you. It'd be a shame if I had to burn down another building."

I go completely still and turn to him with horror as the realization dawns on me.

Jeff chuckles evilly. "Did you really think I wouldn't find you, Jazzy? You belong to me." His eyes turn hard. "It would be a shame if that handsome firefighter of yours perished in a fire. Actually," he cocks his head to the side, "I guess it would be kind of ironic, wouldn't it? Or maybe poetic?"

I shake my head as if I can deny it, but Jeff's grin only widens. "So, we have an understanding? You come home to me —where you belong—and nothing happens to your little firefighter. Okay?"

I don't speak. I just swallow as hollowness settles in the pit of my stomach.

It's bad enough that so many people were already hurt because of me.

I won't let Zeke be another casualty.

See? I knew it was all too good to be true. Good things like Zeke just don't happen to girls like me.

There's always a monster lurking around the corner to drag me back to hell.

Chapter Six

Zeke

I RUSH HOME after containing the fire in a residential neighborhood on the edge of the city. I can't wait to hop in a shower and get back to Jaz.

It's alarming how much I ache just being away from her now. It's like I've found the other half of me, and I no longer feel complete without her.

Actually, no. I've *never* been complete without her. I just didn't know it. I didn't know what I was missing until I laid eyes on her and something inside me just clicked.

She's *everything* to me now.

"Jaz?" I call out her name as soon as I open the

door.

I frown when I don't hear an answer. I already know before I scour the apartment that she's not here.

I can *feel* her lack of presence. There's no electric current, no spark of energy like I usually feel when she's near.

And I pause as it hits me like a ton of bricks.

I don't know *how* I know, but I just *know* something's wrong.

I head back out the door, still covered in soot and ashes. I don't have time to shower. I have to find Jaz.

I head to the diner she works at. Maybe she never told me where she works, but while she was sleeping last night, I did my research.

I stalked her online like a psycho and found out everything there is to know about her. Where she works, when she got her apartment, the year she graduated high school. I even know the time she was born down to the second.

Yeah, I've got it bad.

The diner is bustling with people as I enter. I scan the room for Jaz. My heart drops and panic lights in my chest when I don't see her anywhere.

I head over to the counter and ask for her.

The man behind the counter, whom I can only assume is the manager, frowns when I ask for her. "I don't know where she went, man. She showed up late and then left early without even telling me. As far as I'm concerned, she's fired. You can tell her that if you see her."

A growl of protectiveness rumbles up in my throat, but then a brunette catches my eye.

I decide to leave the manager alone and head over toward her.

She's chewing her bottom lip between her teeth and looking up at me with concerned eyes.

"You're looking for Jaz?" she asks.

"Yes." My heart rate picks up. This girl knows something. I can tell.

"Are you going to hurt her?"

My brow furrows. "Fuck, no! Of course not. I'm trying to help her."

The girl winces at my tone, so I take in a deep breath to attempt to calm myself.

"Look," my eyes flick down to her name badge, "Maria, I would never hurt Jaz. All I want to do is help her, so if you have any idea where she's at, please tell me."

The brunette studies me for another moment, and it takes everything in me to not physically shake her and demand she tell me where Jaz is right this instant. I'm on pins and needles, impatient as fuck, but none of this is her fault, and if I frighten her too much, it might hinder me from finding Jaz.

"A man came in here and dragged her out with him. She didn't look like she wanted to go with him."

My vision blurs as I see red. "Do you know who he was?" my voice comes out as a hoarse croak. My hands ball into fists at the thought of a man forcing Jaz to do anything.

Maria shakes her head before she adds, "No, but he said something about her neglecting her duties as a daughter." I firm my jaw. Jaz's father is dead, so it has to be her stepdad. Although we haven't had time to talk about much, I was able to put two and two together and figure out why she's been scraping by and struggling to be on her own at such a young age.

I thank Maria before turning and heading toward the door. I'm not exactly sure where Jaz is, but I have a pretty good idea of where to start.

I pull out my phone and call up my buddy who's a detective with the local police department. One of the perks of being a firefighter is that we have close contacts within the force. I've never called in a favor like this before, but there's a first time for everything, and Alex knows me. He knows I wouldn't be asking for shit if it wasn't serious.

"Hey man, it's me," I say when he picks up. "I need

your help."

"What's up?" Alex responds.

"I need a favor."

"Alright, shoot."

"I need the address of a guy. Jeff Belamy."

"Got it," Alex says, no questions asked, before he reads the address off to me.

"Thanks, man. I owe you one." I hang up and hail a taxi, offering to pay the guy double if he can get me there within the next ten minutes.

As I ride, my mind races with thoughts of Jaz. When I get my hands on her piece of shit stepdad...

I flex my hands, my nostrils flaring. I can imagine what the man wants with her, and it makes me want to roar with rage.

She's been through so much already, and now this.

I'll tear this fucker limb from limb with my bare hands if he's harmed a hair on her head.

When I arrive at my destination, I hop out of the taxi and throw the driver a hundred. It's more than double what I offered him, but I don't have time to wait around for him to make change.

I don't bother knocking on the door. Instead, I kick it in and go barreling through the house, intent on finding Jaz.

I'm half-crazed with worry. "Jaz!" I call out her name. "Jaz!"

"What the fuck?" A man who I can only assume is her stepfather steps out of a room.

"Where is she?" I growl.

"Who?" he asks.

I can see the fear in his eyes, and I tighten my hold on his throat. Good. He should fear me. If he's hurt one hair on my girl's precious head, I'll demolish him.

"Who?" he chokes out again, playing dumb.

And that just pisses me the fuck off.

I don't have time for this. I wrap my arm around his throat and pull him back, slamming him against the wall. "Where is she?" I repeat, my voice low and dangerous.

"I don't know what you're talking about. I haven't seen her," he coughs, his eyes bulging.

"Where is she?" I ask again, growling.

"F-fine," he stutters. "In there."

He points to the room he just came out of, and I look up just as Jaz's tiny frame fills the doorway.

I push off him and hurry over to Jaz. "Jaz," I breathe out her name in relief as I pull her to me and then hold her out to look over her. "Are you hurt?"

She shakes her head before a sob comes out of her and she throws herself in my arms.

"Ssh," I soothe her as I catch her and hold her against me. "Daddy's got you now. Everything's going to be okay."

She sniffs and pulls back from me. I watch as she looks over my shoulder, her eyes widening in fear.

"Zeke!" she screams my name, and I turn to see Jeff pouring gasoline all over the floor.

What the fuck? Who keeps gasoline on standby in the house? Was this his plan all along? To burn his house down?

I don't even try to reason with the crazy fucker. Instead, I grab Jaz and shield her with my body as I walk us away from her stepdad.

He lets out a maniacal laugh as he lights a match and throws it on the gas.

I feel the heat from the instant flames that surround us. The fucker must have had gas already poured all around his house, and it's an oversight on my part that I didn't smell it as soon as I walked in the door. The only thing I can contribute my lax to is the adrenaline rush of being so worried about Jaz I couldn't think of anything else.

"Zeke!" Jaz is screaming my name, and all I can tell her is to hang on tight as I run us to the door. The heat is so intense it's rising past my waist, and the pain shoots all through my back as my shirt catches fire.

"Zeke, we can't make it out!" Jaz yells as she holds me tighter, her nails digging into my skin.

"Just hang onto me, baby. I've got you."

I don't know where her stepdad is or if he was happy to go down in the flames like the crazy fucker he obviously is, but all I can think about is Jaz.

Jaz.

She's the one I'm trying to save.

She's the one I'm trying to protect.

I'm going to keep her alive.

I look down at her, and her eyes are wide and scared. I push her head against my chest to protect her from the smoke and flames as I pummel my way through to the door, taking the brunt of the heat.

I don't know how long I can last, but I do know I'm not letting go. I run through the door and out into the driveway, pulling her with me.

The flames follow us, enveloping the door we just exited. I fall to my knees as I feel the heat from the flames grazing my back. The pain is something I'm not familiar with, and it's agonizing.

"Zeke!" Jaz yells as my eyes start to close. I'm so exhausted, and the last thing I feel is Jaz's cool tears against my cheek.

And then, there's nothing but darkness.

Chapter Seven

Jaz

I'M NOT ready to lose him. I can't.

I watch as the paramedics rush him onto the stretcher and into the ambulance. I don't even care that my arms and legs hurt from the burns and bruises I got escaping the fire. I need to be taken to the hospital with him. I need to be there when he wakes up.

"Jaz, we're taking care of him. Let us look at you," the paramedic who attended me after my apartment building burnt down begs me, holding onto my arm.

"No, I need to be with Zeke." I pull my arm from his grip and run to the ambulance, jumping inside before the doors are even closed. "I need to be with him."

"Jaz, we're going to take good care of him," the paramedic tells me as he straps a monitor to Zeke's chest and puts a needle in his arm.

"I need to be there. I need to be with him the whole time," I insist as the door to the ambulance is closed. I physically shove the paramedic out of my way and climb over the bench so that I'm sitting next to Zeke.

"Jaz, you need to let us do our job," he insists, placing his hands gently on my shoulders.

I shake him off, not wanting to hear anything he has to say. He needs to take me to the hospital, and I need to be there with Zeke to make sure he's okay.

The paramedic sighs, and I hear him radio the hospital with our arrival. I wait anxiously for the ambulance to turn a corner and begin the drive to the hospital. I lay my head down on Zeke's chest and try to listen to the rhythm of his heart, but it's too faint. I watch as the paramedic checks his pulse, and I know that it's too slow. I watch as his eyes roll back into his head, and I know he's close to death. I watch his body temperature drop and his cheeks get increasingly pale. I'm losing him.

Oh god, I can't lose him. The tears spill down my

cheeks. This is all my fault. All my fault. If it hadn't been for me, none of this would have happened. I should have never left my stepdad's house. I should have just stayed there with him and endured my lot in life.

"Hey, Zeke," I whisper, stroking my fingers down his cheek. "You need to wake up." I swallow as my voice breaks. "Please, for the love of God, wake the fuck up! I'm not supposed to live without you. I *can't* live without you."

I don't know what I'm going to do if I lose him.

He'll make it. He *has* to. I can't bear to think otherwise.

As I sit there, watching the paramedic do everything he can to save Zeke's life, I feel a burning anger build up inside of me. I make a vow to myself right then and there that if Zeke dies—if I lose him—I won't be responsible for my actions. I don't care if I have to kill. If I have to destroy my life, I'll do it. If I have to fucking die, I don't care. I just want him back.

When we finally arrive at the hospital, Zeke is wheeled in by two paramedics. Two more paramedics are standing by the door, blocking me from following.

"No! I need to be with him!" I yell in a panic.

"Calm down, ma'am," one of the paramedics

blocking the door tells me, placing a hand on my shoulder.

"I can't be calm! I need to be with him!" I cry.

"Jaz, let them do their job," the paramedic that rode on the ambulance with me tells me in a gentle voice as he takes my hand. "We'll take you to him as soon as they're done."

As if on cue, one of the paramedics loading Zeke into an elevator speaks, "We're prepared to take Mr. Thompson to surgery right away. We'll do everything we can and call you as soon as he's out of surgery."

I nod, knowing that they won't be able to tell me anything until they know if Zeke will be okay. I'm led into a small waiting room with a couple of chairs and a table in the corner. All of the chairs are full, and people are frantically waiting to hear news on their loved ones. The waiting room is trashed with magazines and cups strewn all over the floor.

I sit down in the corner to wait. Through the double doors, I see a nurse pacing back and forth.

"Excuse me, Nurse," I say, standing up. "Can you please tell me what room Zeke Thompson is in?"

"I'm sorry," the nurse tells me, "Family only."

I press my back up against the wall, sliding down until I'm sitting on the floor. What the fuck am I going to do now? I have no money, no home, and no way of getting to Zeke.

I don't know how long I sit there, but it feels like forever. I'm starving and so thirsty, but I don't dare get up to get food or water. I need to stay here, at least until I know if Zeke will be okay. I just want to know if he's going to make it or not.

I don't know how much more of this I can take. I feel like shit, and I'm just drained. My body shakes in a violent chill, and I'm so cold that I'm almost freezing.

"Hey, are you okay, honey?" an old woman sitting next to me asks.

"Yeah, just a little tired," I lie. "I'm just waiting for my... for my friend to get out of surgery." It seems weird to call Zeke a friend when he's so much more than that, but calling him a boyfriend seems juvenile.

"I see," she says, nodding her head. "Well, I hope everything goes well for you and your friend. It's tough waiting for news like this, but you've got to stay strong."

I give her a weak smile and nod, grateful for her kind words. But deep down, I know I'm not strong enough. I'm falling apart, and I can't keep it together much longer.

Hours pass before I finally get news on Zeke. The

doctor comes out and calls my name, and I jump up, heart racing.

"Ms. Johnson?" he asks, and I nod. "I'm pleased to say that Mr. Thompson made it through surgery. It was touch and go for a while there, but we managed to repair the damage. He came out of recovery just fine, and he's asking for you. Do you have any questions?"

I shake my head, unable to find my voice. Tears stream down my face as relief washes over me. Zeke's going to be okay.

Still, I need the assurance. "So, he's going to be okay?"

The doctor smiles at me kindly. "I think he'll be just fine. He's a tough one."

My shoulders sag in relief. "Can I see him now?" The doctor nods and motions for me to follow him.

I enter the hospital room and see Zeke lying on the bed, hooked up to various machines. His face is pale, and there are burns all over his body, but he's alive, and somehow, he still looks so big and strong. I walk over to him and take his hand, tears still streaming down my face.

"Hey," he whispers, giving my hand a weak squeeze. "Don't cry, baby. It's okay. I'm fine."

He's running his hands all along my face and

down my body. "Are you okay? I heard you wouldn't let the paramedics look you over." He's frowning at me in disapproval now.

"I'm fine," I say, trying to sound strong even though my voice is shaking. "Oh, Zeke, I was so scared. I thought I was going to lose you."

"You won't lose me that easily," he says, managing a small smile. "There's no way I'm leaving you, baby." His voice drops a notch. "You need your daddy, don't you?"

And just like that, my body is on fire for him.

"Zeke..." my voice comes out breathy.

Zeke grabs the back of my neck and pulls me down to press his lips against mine.

He kisses me like a starving man, his tongue ravishing my mouth. I'm instantly wet and throbbing for him, even though I know this isn't the time or the place.

Eventually, Zeke pulls back, breaking the kiss, his breathing ragged.

"Listen, Jaz, there's something I need to tell you," he says, his voice serious.

"What is it?" I ask, suddenly feeling a sense of dread at the seriousness in his tone.

"I love you, Jaz," he says, looking directly into my eyes. "I know we haven't known each other for that long, but, baby, you're *it* for me. I can't imagine my life without you."

He cups my face in the palm of his hand. "Say you'll be mine, sweetheart. Let me take care of you forever. No more scraping by and killing yourself at dead-end jobs. I've got you. I want you to be happy. If you want to work, that's fine, but find something you love to do. You're too young to be doing all this stressing. Just let your daddy take care of you."

My heart swells at his words, and I feel tears prick at the corners of my eyes again, this time from happiness. "I love you too, Zeke," I confess. "You make me happier than I ever thought it was possible to be."

I nuzzle my face into his neck, kissing his neck and burying my face in the crook of his shoulder.

"Fuck," he grunts, his voice suddenly sounding strained. "Jaz, if you don't stop that, I'm going to fuck you right here on this hospital bed."

I pull back, my face flaming even as my core throbs at the thought, but Zeke has to be in pain and exhausted, and here I am all over him.

I lean back. "I'm sorry," I say apologetically. "I know you're hurt—"

I never get a chance to finish my sentence because Zeke grabs me and pulls me so that I'm straddling him on the hospital bed.

"Zeke! What about your burns?" I gently touch one of the bandages on his chest.

"Doesn't ache as bad as my cock, baby," he says as he settles me on top of his swollen length.

"Zeke..." My protest turns into a moan as Zeke's fingers find their way under my dress and pull my panties to the side.

"I'm going to fuck you so hard, baby," he says, his voice gruffer than I've ever heard him. "I'm going to make you scream my name so loud, the people in the next county will hear."

He guides his cock to my entrance, and I'm so wet I easily slide down on his length. I forget where we are. I suddenly don't care that we're in a hospital.

The monitors Zeke are hooked up to are going crazy as he pushes the tip of his swollen length inside me. With an irritated growl, Zeke rips the IV and sensors from his body.

And then we don't move.

Zeke just sits there and stares into my eyes. All the tension and anxiety I've been feeling since Jeff physically pulled me from my job is gone, replaced with a feeling of completeness. I feel like I could float away. I wonder if I'm in a dream.

"Fuck, I love you, Jaz," he says.

And then, with a groan and a thrust of his hips,

we're joined.

Once more, I scream his name as if it were my last breath, and it feels like it is. I feel like I'm swept up in a tornado of fucking Zeke.

I cry out again as Zeke pulls me closer to him.

"Ride me, baby," he growls, positioning my hips so that he's as deep inside me as he can be.

I do as I'm told, clamping my pussy so tight around his cock that I know he can feel every inch of me.

He keeps his eyes locked on mine. His gaze is like a physical touch, so full of love and desire, it only intensifies the feeling of his cock inside me.

He lifts me off of his prick, only to slam me back down over his length. I cry out again at the force of his thrust, but it only makes me clench around him tighter.

I'm so close. I feel like I'm flying already, with Zeke still deep inside me.

I'm not even thinking, I'm just feeling when Zeke pulls me down on top of him and flips me over.

I'm up on my knees, my arms outstretched in front of me, trying to stabilize myself before Zeke fills me again. He's gripping my hips so tight, I know there will be bruises.

I didn't even notice before, but Zeke's bed is in an

L-shape, so his hips are on a slight angle with mine. I can feel him even deeper when he thrusts into me from behind like this.

I cry out again as Zeke's hands grip my ass, pulling me back on his cock. His other hand is still on my hips, pushing me back on his cock until I feel his balls slapping against my soaking clit.

I can feel my orgasm coming. It feels like it's behind a closed door, and I'm beating against it, trying to get in.

I feel the warning drip of cum from Zeke's cock, and I know he's close too.

"Come for me, Jaz," he growls. "Show your daddy how much you love this cock inside your pussy."

And that's all it takes. I feel my barriers implode, and I'm soaring. My pussy clenches around Zeke's cock, milking it for all it's got. I can feel his cock throbbing inside me, shooting his cum into my hungry pussy.

I lean back, still impaled on Zeke's cock, and he wraps his arms around me, his lips on my shoulder.

We ride our orgasms out until there's nothing left but Zeke's cock still inside me.

He finally rolls me over and collapses on the hospital bed, pulling me on top of him.

And we fall asleep just like that.

Epilogue

One Year Later

Zeke

MY HEART RACES as I enter the room. The scent of love hangs heavily in the air, and I feel my body become more alive with every breath I take. Jaz is already here, and I can feel her eyes on me as I approach. I can feel the heat between us, the desire and the anticipation. I can feel the electricity that's crackling in the air, and I mentally thank whatever deity is out there again for the wonder that is my wife.

We only waited a month before I married her. I

knew I wanted to spend the rest of my life with her, and she did likewise, so we didn't see the point in waiting.

Life is too short.

I'm still a firefighter, and though I know it worries Jaz every time I have to respond to an emergency, it's my calling, and she understands that.

As for her part, she decided to turn the room I gifted her with into a studio.

Turns out my little girl is a talented artist, and I couldn't be more thrilled. I'd be lying if I said that I don't love that Jaz is doing something that makes it so she can stay at home where I know she's safe at all times.

And mine. All mine.

And I can't wait to make her mine all over again. I take her every night like it's the first time, but somehow it gets better and better every time.

I think it's because I fall more and more in love with her every day.

I take a few steps toward her, and she smiles up at me, her eyes twinkling with mischief. I reach out and take her hand, bringing it to my lips as I meet her gaze. She smiles, and I can see the pleasure there, the desire and the unspoken understanding of what we are about to do.

We stand there for a moment, just looking into each other's eyes, sending unspoken words through our gaze. Without a word, I lead her to the bed, my heart pounding in my chest. I can feel the anticipation and excitement growing as we slowly undress each other.

Our clothes drift to the floor and our bodies come together in perfect harmony, our skin touching and creating a beautiful sensation between us. I can feel the love and the passion between us as we move together. The desire and pleasure builds up inside us with each caress and kiss.

We lay down on the bed, and I position myself between her legs and pull her closer to me. She wraps her arms around me and holds me tight as I start to move my body, pressing into her and exploring her curves. I can feel her heat and her softness. I lift my head and look into her eyes as I start to move my body in a slow and tantalizing rhythm.

My mouth moves down her body, exploring her curves and her softness. I kiss her breasts, and I can feel her heart pounding beneath my lips.

Fuck, this woman is perfect.

I continue to move my body in a circle, teasing her and exploring her body with my tongue. I can feel her muscles tense up as she starts to get aroused, her breathing becoming quicker and deeper. I taste the excitement on her lips as she moans, and my cock jumps in response, a bead of precum leaking out of the tip.

My lips move further down her body, worshipping her with my mouth. I move my hands up and down her body, exploring every inch of her as I kiss her in an ever-deepening intensity.

My tongue moves in circles around her clitoris, sending wave after wave of pleasure through her body. I can feel her body quivering and shaking beneath me as she starts to come undone.

"That's it, baby," I encourage her. "Come all over your husband's face."

As I continue to lap at her folds, I feel her orgasm start to build up inside her until it finally erupts, sending a wave of pleasure coursing through her. Her body arches against my mouth, her fingers spearing into my hair. My chest swells knowing that I put her in such a beautiful state of ecstasy.

I crawl up beside her and gather her into my arms. We lay there for a few moments, just breathing and basking in the afterglow. My cock is still hard as granite, precum leaking steadily from my tip.

When Jaz finally reaches for me, her tiny hand circling my aching length, I know she's ready for me.

"Zeke," she purrs my name in my ear, and my cock jumps in her hand.

Fuck, I can't wait any longer.

I move up and position myself between her legs. Taking my time, I enter her. Our bodies become one, our movements perfectly in sync. I reach down and caress her body as I thrust deeper, exploring her depths until we are both taken over by the intensity of it all.

Our bodies move together in an ever-increasing intensity, the pleasure growing until it becomes a wave that we can't contain. I can feel the electricity between us, the passion and the love, and I know that this is something that can never be replaced. We peak together in an incredible moment of ecstasy, and I can feel the joy and the pleasure that comes with it.

As we lay there afterward, our love pulses between us like a live thing.

"I love you," she whispers as she drifts off to sleep.

I plant a gentle kiss on her forehead as I stroke her hair away from her face.

"I love you too, Jaz."

This woman is my life and my future, and I'll do anything for her.

She's my *obsession*.

. . .

Want more Emma Bray? Get a FREE book when you sign up here: www.authoremmabray.com.

www.ingramcontent.com/pod-product-compliance
Lightning Source LLC
Chambersburg PA
CBHW021344160726
47994CB00007B/2843